THE POOL OF THE BLACK ONE

BY

ROBERT E. HOWARD

British Library Cataloguing-in-Publication Data
A catalogue record for this book is available from the
British Library

Contents

Robert E. Howard

Robert Ervin Howard was born in Peaster, Texas in 1906. During his youth, his family moved between a variety of Texan boomtowns, and Howard – a bookish and somewhat introverted child – was steeped in the violent myths and legends of the Old South. Although he loved reading and learning, Howard developed a distinctly Texan, hardboiled outlook on the world. He became a passionate fan of boxing, taking it up at an amateur level, and from the age of nine began to write adventure tales of semi-historical bloodshed. In 1919, when Howard was thirteen, his family moved to the Central Texas hamlet of Cross Plains, where he would stay for the rest of his life.

At fifteen Howard began to read the pulp magazines of the day, and to write more seriously. The December 1922 issue of his high school newspaper featured two of his stories, 'Golden Hope Christmas' and 'West is West'. In 1924 he sold his first piece – a short caveman tale titled 'Spear and Fang' – for $16 to the not-yet-famous *Weird Tales* magazine. He published with the magazine regularly over the next few years. 1929 was a breakout year for Howard, in that the 23-year-old writer began to sell to other magazines, such as *Ghost Stories* and *Argosy*, both of whom had previously sent him hundreds of rejection slips. In 1930, he began a correspondence with weird fiction master H. P. Lovecraft which ran up to his death six years later, and is regarded as one of the great correspondence cycles in all of fantasy literature.

It was partly due to Lovecraft's encouragement that Howard created his most famous character, Conan the Cimmerian. Conan – a barbarian-turned-King during the Hyborian Age, a mythical period of some 12,000 years ago – featured in seventeen *Weird Tales* stories between 1933 and 1936, and is now regarded as having spawned the 'sword and sorcery' genre, making Howard's influence on fantasy literature comparable to that of J. R. R. Tolkien's. The Conan stories have since been adapted many times, most famously in the series of films starring Arnold Schwarzenegger.

Howard was enjoying an all-time high in sales by the beginning of 1936, but he was also deeply upset by the ill health of his mother, who had fallen into a coma. On the morning of June 11, 1936, he asked an attending nurse whether she would ever recover, and the nurse replied negatively. Howard walked to his car, parked outside the family home in Cross Plains, and shot himself. He died eight hours later, aged just thirty.

CHAPTER I

Into the west, unknown of man,
Ships have sailed since the world began.
Read, if you dare, what Skelos wrote,
With dead hands fumbling his silken coat;
And follow the ships through the wind-blown wrack
Follow the ships that come not back.

Sancha, once of Kordava, yawned daintily, stretched her supple limbs luxuriously, and composed herself more comfortably on the ermine-fringed silk spread on the carack's poop-deck. That the crew watched her with burning interest from waist and forecastle she was lazily aware, just as she was also aware that her short silk kirtle veiled little of her voluptuous contours from their eager eyes. Wherefore she smiled insolently and prepared to snatch a few more winks before the sun, which was just thrusting his golden disk above the ocean, should dazzle her eyes.

But at that instant a sound reached her ears unlike the creaking of timbers, thrum of cordage and lap of waves. She sat up, her gaze fixed on the rail, over which, to her amazement, a dripping figure clambered. Her dark eyes opened wide, her red lips parted in an O of surprize. The intruder was a stranger to her. Water ran in rivulets from his great shoulders and down his heavy arms. His single garment—a pair of bright crimson silk breeks—was soaking wet, as was his broad gold-buckled girdle and the sheathed sword it supported. As he stood at the rail, the rising sun etched him like a great bronze statue. He ran his fingers through his streaming black mane, and his blue eyes lit as they rested on the girl.

"Who are you?" she demanded. "Whence did you come?"

He made a gesture toward the sea that took in a whole quarter of the compass, while his eyes did not leave her supple figure.

"Are you a merman, that you rise up out of the sea?" she asked, confused by the candor of his gaze, though she was accustomed to admiration.

Before he could reply, a quick step sounded on the boards, and the master of the carack was glaring at the stranger, fingers twitching at sword-hilt.

"Who the devil are you, sirrah?" this one demanded in no friendly tone.

"I am Conan," the other answered imperturbably. Sancha pricked up her ears anew; she had never heard Zingaran spoken with such an accent as the stranger spoke it.

"And how did you get aboard my ship?" The voice grated with suspicion.

"I swam."

"Swam!" exclaimed the master angrily. "Dog, would you jest with me? We are far beyond sight of land. Whence do you come?"

Conan pointed with a muscular brown arm toward the east, banded in dazzling gold by the lifting sun.

"I came from the Islands."

"Oh!" The other regarded him with increased interest. Black brows drew down over scowling eyes, and the thin lip lifted unpleasantly.

"So you are one of those dogs of the Barachans."

A faint smile touched Conan's lips.

"And do you know who I am?" his questioner demanded.

"This ship is the Wastrel; so you must be Zaporavo."

"Aye!" It touched the captain's grim vanity that the man should know him. He was a tall man, tall as Conan, though of leaner build. Framed in his steel morion his face was dark, saturnine and hawk-like, wherefore men called him the Hawk. His armor and garments were rich and ornate, after the fashion of a Zingaran grandee. His hand was never far from his sword-hilt.

There was little favor in the gaze he bent on Conan. Little love was lost between Zingaran renegades and the outlaws who infested the Baracha Islands off the southern coast of Zingara. These men were mostly sailors from Argos, with a sprinkling of other nationalities. They raided the shipping, and harried the Zingaran coast towns, just as the Zingaran buccaneers did, but these dignified their profession by calling themselves Freebooters, while they dubbed the Barachans pirates. They were neither the first nor the last to gild the name of thief.

Some of these thoughts passed through Zaporavo's mind as he toyed with his sword-hilt and scowled at his uninvited guest. Conan gave no hint of what his own thoughts might be. He stood with folded arms as placidly as if upon his own deck; his lips smiled and his eyes were untroubled.

"What are you doing here?" the Freebooter demanded abruptly.

"I found it necessary to leave the rendezvous at Tortage before moonrise last night," answered Conan. "I departed in a leaky boat, and rowed and bailed all night. Just at dawn I saw your topsails, and left the miserable tub to sink, while I made better speed in the water."

"There are sharks in these waters," growled Zaporavo, and was vaguely irritated by the answering shrug of the mighty shoulders. A glance toward the waist showed a screen of eager faces staring upward. A word would send them leaping up on the poop in a storm of swords that would overwhelm even such a fightingman as the stranger looked to be.

"Why should I burden myself with every nameless vagabond that the sea casts up?" snarled Zaporavo, his look and manner more insulting than his words.

"A ship can always use another good sailor," answered the other without resentment. Zaporavo scowled, knowing the truth of that assertion. He hesitated, and doing so, lost his ship, his command, his girl, and his life. But of course he could not see into the future, and to him Conan was only another wastrel, cast up, as he put it, by the sea. He did not like the man; yet the fellow had given him no provocation. His manner was not insolent, though rather more confident than Zaporavo liked to see.

"You'll work for your keep," snarled the Hawk. "Get off the poop. And remember, the only law here is my will."

The smile seemed to broaden on Conan's thin lips. Without hesitation but without haste he turned and descended into the waist. He did not look again at Sancha, who, during the brief conversation, had watched eagerly, all eyes and ears.

As he came into the waist the crew thronged about him Zingarans, all of them, half naked, their gaudy silk garments splashed with tar, jewels glinting in ear-rings and dagger-hilts. They were eager for the time-honored sport of baiting the stranger. Here he would be tested, and his future status in the crew decided. Up on the poop Zaporavo had apparently already forgotten the stranger's existence,

7

but Sancha watched, tense with interest. She had become familiar with such scenes, and knew the baiting would be brutal and probably bloody.

But her familiarity with such matters was scanty compared to that of Conan. He smiled faintly as he came into the waist and saw the menacing figures pressing truculently about him. He paused and eyed the ring inscrutably, his composure unshaken. There was a certain code about these things. If he had attacked the captain, the whole crew would have been at his throat, but they would give him a fair chance against the one selected to push the brawl.

The man chosen for this duty thrust himself forward—a wiry brute, with a crimson sash knotted about his head like a turban. His lean chin jutted out, his scarred face was evil beyond belief. Every glance, each swaggering movement was an affront. His way of beginning the baiting was as primitive, raw and crude as himself.

"Baracha, eh?" he sneered. "That's where they raise dogs for men. We of the Fellowship spit on 'em—like this!"

He spat in Conan's face and snatched at his own sword.

The Barachan's movement was too quick for the eye to follow. His sledge-like fist crunched with a terrible impact against his tormentor's jaw, and the Zingaran catapulted through the air and fell in a crumpled heap by the rail.

Conan turned towards the others. But for a slumbering glitter in his eyes, his bearing was unchanged. But the baiting was over as suddenly as it had begun. The seamen lifted their companion; his broken jaw hung slack, his head lolled unnaturally.

"By Mitra, his neck's broken!" swore a black-bearded searogue.

"You Freebooters are a weak-boned race," laughed the pirate. "On the Barachas we take no account of such taps as that. Will you play at sword-strokes, now, any of you? No? Then all's well, and we're friends, eh?"

There were plenty of tongues to assure him that he spoke truth. Brawny arms swung the dead man over the rail, and a dozen fins cut the water as he sank. Conan laughed and spread his mighty arms as a great cat might stretch itself, and his gaze sought the deck above. Sancha leaned over the rail, red lips parted, dark eyes aglow with interest. The sun behind her outlined her lithe figure through the light kirtle which its glow made transparent. Then across her fell Zaporavo's scowling shadow and a heavy hand fell possessively on her slim shoulder. There were menace and meaning in the glare he bent on the man in the waist; Conan grinned back, as if at a jest none knew but himself.

Zaporavo made the mistake so many autocrats make; alone in somber grandeur on the poop, he underestimated the man below him. He had his opportunity to kill Conan, and he let it pass, engrossed in his own gloomy ruminations. He did not find it easy to think any of the dogs beneath his feet constituted a menace to him. He had stood in the high places so long, and had ground so many foes underfoot, that he unconsciously assumed himself to be above the machinations of inferior rivals.

Conan, indeed, gave him no provocation. He mixed with the crew, lived and made merry as they did. He proved himself a skilled sailor, and by far the strongest man any of them had seen. He did the work of three men, and was always first to spring to any heavy or dangerous task. His mates began to rely upon him. He did not quarrel with them, and they were careful not to quarrel with him. He gambled with them, putting up his girdle and sheath for a stake, won their money and weapons, and gave them back with a laugh. The crew instinctively looked toward him as the leader of the forecastle. He vouchsafed no information as to what had caused him to flee the Barachas, but the knowledge that he was capable of a deed bloody enough to have exiled him from that wild band increased the respect felt toward him by the fierce Freebooters. Toward Zaporavo and the mates he was imperturbably courteous, never insolent or servile.

The dullest was struck by the contrast between the harsh, taciturn, gloomy commander, and the pirate whose laugh was gusty and ready, who roared ribald songs in a dozen languages, guzzled ale like a toper, and—apparently—had no thought for the morrow.

Had Zaporavo known he was being compared, even though unconsciously, with a man before the mast, he would have been speechless with amazed anger. But he was engrossed with his broodings, which had become blacker and grimmer as the years crawled by, and with his vague grandiose dreams; and with the girl whose possession was a bitter pleasure, just as all his pleasures were.

And she looked more and more at the black-maned giant who towered among his mates at work or play. He never spoke to her, but there was no mistaking the candor of his gaze. She did not mistake it, and she wondered if she dared the perilous game of leading him on.

No great length of time lay between her and the palaces of Kordava, but it was as if a world of change separated her from the life she had lived before Zaporavo tore her screaming from the flaming caravel his wolves had plundered. She, who had been the spoiled and petted daughter of the Duke of Kordava, learned what it was to be a buccaneer's plaything, and because she was supple enough to bend without breaking, she lived where other women had died, and because she was young and vibrant with life, she came to find pleasure in the existence.

The life was uncertain, dream-like, with sharp contrasts of battle, pillage, murder, and flight. Zaporavo's red visions made it even more uncertain than that of the average Freebooter. No one knew what he planned next. Now they had left all charted coasts behind and were plunging further and further into that unknown billowy waste ordinarily shunned by seafarers, and into which, since the beginnings of Time, ships had ventured, only to vanish from the sight of man for ever. All known lands lay behind them, and day upon day the blue surging immensity lay empty to their sight. Here there was no loot—no towns to sack nor ships to burn. The men murmured, though they did not let their murmurings reach the ears of their implacable master, who tramped the poop day and night in gloomy majesty, or pored over ancient charts and time-yellowed maps, reading in tomes that were crumbling masses of worm-eaten parchment. At times he talked to Sancha, wildly it seemed to her, of lost continents, and fabulous isles dreaming unguessed amidst the blue foam of nameless gulfs, where horned dragons guarded treasures gathered by pre-human kings, long, long ago.

Sancha listened, uncomprehending, hugging her slim knees, her thoughts constantly roving away from the words of her grim companion back to a clean-limbed bronze giant whose laughter was gusty and elemental as the sea wind.

So, after many weary weeks, they raised land to westward, and at dawn dropped anchor in a shallow bay, and saw a beach which was like a white band bordering an expanse of gently grassy slopes, masked by green trees.

The wind brought scents of fresh vegetation and spices, and Sancha clapped her hands with glee at the prospect of adventuring ashore. But her eagerness turned to sulkiness when Zaporavo ordered her to remain aboard until he sent for her. He never gave any explanation for his commands; so she never knew his reason, unless it was the lurking devil in him that frequently made him hurt her without cause.

So she lounged sulkily on the poop and watched the men row ashore through the calm water that sparkled like liquid jade in the morning sunlight. She saw them bunch together on the sands, suspicious, weapons ready, while several scattered out through the trees that fringed the beach. Among these, she noted, was Conan. There was no mistaking that tall brown figure with its springy step. Men said he was no civilized man at all, but a Cimmerian, one of those barbaric tribesmen who dwelt in the gray hills of the far North, and whose raids struck terror in their southern neighbors. At least, she knew that there was something about him, some super-vitality or barbarism that set him apart from his wild mates.

Voices echoed along the shore, as the silence reassured the buccaneers. The clusters broke up, as men scattered along the beach in search of fruit. She saw them climbing and plucking among the trees, and her pretty mouth watered. She stamped a little foot and swore with a proficiency acquired by association with her blasphemous companions.

The men on shore had indeed found fruit, and were gorging on it, finding one unknown golden-skinned variety especially luscious. But Zaporavo did not seek or eat fruit. His scouts having found nothing indicating men or beasts in the neighborhood, he stood staring inland, at the long reaches of grassy slopes melting into one another. Then, with a brief word, he shifted his sword-belt and strode in under the trees. His mate expostulated with him against going alone, and was rewarded by a savage blow in the mouth. Zaporavo had his reasons for wishing to go alone. He desired to learn if this island were indeed that mentioned in the mysterious Book of Skelos, whereon, nameless sages aver, strange monsters guard crypts filled with hieroglyph-careen gold. Nor, for murky reasons of his own, did he wish to share his knowledge, if it were true, with any one, much less his own crew.

Sancha, watching eagerly from the poop, saw him vanish into the leafy fastness. Presently she saw Conan, the Barachan, turn, glance briefly at the men scattered up and down the beach; then the pirate went quickly in the direction taken by Zaporavo, and likewise vanished among the trees.

Sancha's curiosity was piqued. She waited for them to reappear, but they did not. The seamen still moved aimlessly up and down the beach, and some had wandered inland. Many had lain down in the shade to sleep. Time passed and she fidgeted about restlessly. The sun began to beat down hotly, in spite of the canopy above the poop-deck. Here it was warm, silent, draggingly monotonous; a few yards away across a band of blue shallow water, the cool shady mystery of tree-fringed beach and woodland-dotted meadow beckoned her. Moreover, the mystery concerning Zaporavo and Conan tempted her.

She well knew the penalty for disobeying her merciless master, and she sat for some time, squirming with indecision. At last she decided that it was worth even one of Zaporavo's whippings to play truant, and with no more ado she kicked off her soft leather sandals, slipped out of her kirtle and stood up on the deck naked as Eve. Clambering over the rail and down the chains, she slid into the water and swam ashore. She stood on the beach a few moments, squirming as the sands tickled her small toes, while she looked for the crew. She saw only a few, at some distance up or down the beach. Many were fast asleep under the trees, bits of golden fruit still clutched in their fingers. She wondered why they should sleep so soundly, so early in the day.

None hailed her as she crossed the white girdle of sand and entered the shade of the woodland. The trees, she found, grew in irregular clusters, and between these groves stretched rolling expanses of meadow-like slopes. As she progressed inland, in the direction taken by Zaporavo, she was entranced by the green vistas that unfolded gently before her, soft slope beyond slope, carpeted with green sward and dotted with groves. Between the slopes lay gentle declivities, likewise swarded. The scenery seemed to melt into itself, or each scene into the other; the view was singular, at once broad and restricted. Over all a dreamy silence lay like an enchantment.

Then she came suddenly onto the level summit of a slope, circled with tall trees, and the dreamily faery-like sensation vanished abruptly at the sight of what lay on the reddened and trampled grass. Sancha involuntarily cried out and recoiled, then stole forward, wide-eyed, trembling in every limb.

It was Zaporavo who lay there on the sward, staring sightlessly upward, a gaping wound in his breast. His sword lay near his nerveless hand. The Hawk had made his last swoop.

It is not to be said that Sancha gazed on the corpse of her lord without emotion. She had no cause to love him, yet she felt at least the sensation any girl might feel when looking on the body of the man who was first to possess her. She did not weep or feel any need of weeping, but she was seized by a strong trembling, her blood seemed to congeal briefly, and she resisted a wave of hysteria.

She looked about her for the man she expected to see. Nothing met her eyes but the ring of tall, thickly leafed forest giants, and the blue slopes beyond them. Had the

Freebooter's slayer dragged himself away, mortally wounded? No bloody tracks led away from the body.

Puzzled, she swept the surrounding trees, stiffening as she caught a rustle in the emerald leaves that seemed not to be of the wind. She went toward the trees, staring into the leafy depths.

"Conan?" Her call was inquiring; her voice sounded strange and small in the vastness of silence that had grown suddenly tense.

Her knees began to tremble as a nameless panic swept over her.

"Conan!" she cried desperately. "It is I—Sancha! Where are you? Please, Conan—" Her voice faltered away. Unbelieving horror dilated her brown eyes. Her red lips parted to an inarticulate scream. Paralysis gripped her limbs; where she had such desperate need of swift flight, she could not move. She could only shriek wordlessly.

CHAPTER II

When Conan saw Zaporavo stalk alone into the woodland, he felt that the chance he had watched for had come. He had eaten no fruit, nor joined in the horse-play of his mates; all his faculties were occupied with watching the buccaneer chief. Accustomed to Zaporavo's moods, his men were not particularly surprised that their captain should choose to explore an unknown and probably hostile isle alone. They turned to their own amusement, and did not notice Conan when he glided like a stalking panther after the chieftain.

Conan did not underrate his dominance of the crew. But he had not gained the right, through battle and foray, to challenge the captain to a duel to the death. In these empty seas there had been no opportunity for him to prove himself according to Freebooter law. The crew would stand solidly against him if he attacked the chieftain openly. But he knew that if he killed Zaporavo without their knowledge, the leaderless crew would not be likely to be swayed by loyalty to a dead man. In such wolf-packs only the living counted.

So he followed Zaporavo with sword in hand and eagerness in his heart, until he came out onto a level summit, circled with tall trees, between whose trunks he saw the green vistas of the slopes melting into the blue distance. In the midst of the glade Zaporavo, sensing pursuit, turned, hand on hilt.

The buccaneer swore.

"Dog, why do you follow me?"

"Are you mad, to ask?" laughed Conan, coming swiftly toward his erstwhile chief. His lips smiled, and in his blue eyes danced a wild gleam.

Zaporavo ripped out his sword with a black curse, and steel clashed against steel as the Barachan came in recklessly and wide open, his blade singing a wheel of blue flame about his head.

Zaporavo was the veteran of a thousand fights by sea and by land. There was no man in the world more deeply and thoroughly versed than he in the lore of swordcraft. But he had never been pitted against a blade wielded by thews bred in the wild lands beyond the borders of civilization. Against his fighting-craft was matched blinding speed and strength impossible to a civilized man. Conan's manner of fighting was unorthodox, but instinctive and natural as that of a timber wolf. The intricacies of the sword were as useless against his primitive fury as a human boxer's skill against the onslaughts of a panther.

Fighting as he had never fought before, straining every last ounce of effort to parry the blade that flickered like lightning about his head, Zaporavo in desperation caught a full stroke near his hilt, and felt his whole arm go numb beneath the terrific impact. That stroke was instantly followed by a thrust with such terrible drive behind it that the sharp point ripped through chain-mail and ribs like paper, to transfix the heart beneath. Zaporavo's lips writhed in brief agony, but, grim to the last, he made no sound. He was dead before his body relaxed on the trampled grass, where blood drops glittered like spilt rubies in the sun.

Conan shook the red drops from his sword, grinned with unaffected pleasure, stretched like a huge cat—and abruptly stiffened, the expression of satisfaction on his face being replaced by a stare of bewilderment. He stood like a statue, his sword trailing in his hand.

As he lifted his eyes from his vanquished foe, they had absently rested on the surrounding trees, and the vistas beyond. And he had seen a fantastic thing—a thing incredible and inexplicable. Over the soft rounded green shoulder of a distant slope had loped a tall black naked figure, bearing on its shoulder an equally naked white form. The apparition vanished as suddenly as it had appeared, leaving the watcher gasping in surprise.

The pirate stared about him, glanced uncertainly back the way he had come, and swore. He was nonplussed—a bit upset, if the term might be applied to one of such steely nerves as his. In the midst of realistic, if exotic surroundings, a vagrant image of fantasy and nightmare had been introduced. Conan doubted neither his eyesight nor his sanity. He had seen something alien and uncanny, he knew; the mere fact of a black figure racing across the landscape carrying a white captive was bizarre enough, but this black figure had been unnaturally tall.

Shaking his head doubtfully, Conan started off in the direction in which he had seen the thing. He did not argue the wisdom of his move; with his curiosity so piqued, he had no choice but to follow its promptings.

Slope after slope he traversed, each with its even sward and clustered groves. The general trend was always upward, though he ascended and descended the gentle inclines with monotonous regularity. The array of rounded shoulders and shallow declivities was bewildering and apparently endless. But at last he advanced up what he believed was the highest summit on the island, and halted at the sight of green shining walls and towers, which, until he had reached the spot on which he then stood, had merged so perfectly with the green landscape as to be invisible, even to his keen sight.

He hesitated, fingered his sword, then went forward, bitten by the worm of curiosity. He saw no one as he approached a tall archway in the curving wall. There was no door. Peering warily through, he saw what seemed to be a broad open court, grass-carpeted, surrounded by a circular wall of the green semitranslucent substance. Various arches opened from it. Advancing on the balls of his bare feet, sword ready, he chose one of these arches at random, and passed into another similar court. Over an inner wall he saw the pinnacles of strangely shaped towerlike structures. One of these towers was built in, or projected into the court in which he found himself, and a broad stair led up to it, along the side of the wall. Up this he went, wondering if it were all real, or if he were not in the midst of a black lotus dream.

At the head of the stair he found himself on a walled ledge, or balcony, he was not sure which. He could now make out more details of the towers, but they were meaningless to him. He realized uneasily that no ordinary human beings could have built them. There was symmetry about their architecture, and system, but it was a mad symmetry, a system alien to human sanity. As for the plan of the whole town, castle, or whatever it was intended for, he could see just enough to get the impression of a great number of courts, mostly circular, each surrounded by its own wall, and connected with the others by open arches, and all, apparently, grouped about the cluster of fantastic towers in the center.

Turning in the other direction from these towers, he got a fearful shock, and crouched down suddenly behind the parapet of the balcony, glaring amazedly.

The balcony or ledge was higher than the opposite wall, and he was looking over that wall into another swarded court. The inner curve of the further wall of that court differed from the others he had seen, in that, instead of being smooth, it seemed to be banded with long lines or ledges, crowded with small objects the nature of which he could not determine.

However, he gave little heed to the wall at the time. His attention was centered on the band of beings that squatted about a dark green pool in the midst of the court. These creatures were black and naked, made like men, but the least of them, standing upright, would have towered head and shoulders above the tall pirate. They were rangy rather than massive, but were finely formed, with no suggestion of deformity or abnomality, save as their great height was abnormal. But even at that distance Conan sensed the basic diabolism of their features.

In their midst, cringing and naked, stood a youth that Conan recognized as the youngest sailor aboard the Wastrel. He, then, had been the captive the pirate had seen borne across the grass-covered slope. Conan had heard no sound of fighting—saw no blood-stains or wounds on the sleek ebon limbs of the giants. Evidently the lad had wandered inland away from his companions and been snatched up by a black man lurking in ambush. Conan mentally termed the creatures black men, for lack of a better term; instinctively he knew that these tall ebony beings were not men, as he understood the term.

No sound came to him. The blacks nodded and gestured to one another, but they did not seem to speak—vocally, at least. One, squatting on his haunches before the cringing boy, held a pipe-like thing in his hand. This he set to his lips, and apparently blew, though Conan heard no sound. But the Zingaran youth heard or felt, and cringed. He quivered and writhed as if in agony; a regularity became evident in the twitching of his limbs, which quickly became rhythmic. The twitching became a violent jerking, the jerking regular movements. The youth began to dance, as cobras dance by compulsion to the tune of the faquir's fife. There was naught of zest or joyful abandon in that dance. There was, indeed, abandon that was awful to see, but it was not joyful. It was as if the mute tune of the pipes grasped the boy's inmost soul with salacious fingers and with brutal torture wrung from it every involuntary expression of secret passion. It was a convulsion of obscenity, a spasm of lasciviousness— an exudation of secret hungers framed by compulsion: desire without pleasure, pain mated awfully to lust. It was like watching a soul stripped naked, and all its dark and unmentionable secrets laid bare.

Conan glared frozen with repulsion and shaken with nausea. Himself as cleanly elemental as a timber wolf, he was yet not ignorant of the perverse secrets of rotting civilizations. He had roamed the cities of Zamora, and known the women of Shadizar the Wicked. But he sensed here a cosmic vileness transcending mere human degeneracy—a perverse branch on the tree of Life, developed along lines outside human comprehension. It was not at the agonized contortions and posturing of the wretched boy that he was shocked, but at the cosmic obscenity of these beings which could drag to light the abysmal secrets that sleep in the unfathomed darkness of the human soul, and find pleasure in the brazen flaunting of such things as should not be hinted at, even in restless nightmares.

Suddenly the black torturer laid down the pipes and rose, towering over the writhing white figure. Brutally grasping the boy by neck and haunch, the giant up-ended him and thrust him head-first into the green pool. Conan saw the white glimmer of his naked body amid the green water, as the black giant held his captive deep under the surface. Then there was a restless movement among the other blacks, and Conan ducked quickly below the balcony wall, not daring to raise his head lest he be seen.

After a while his curiosity got the better of him, and he cautiously peered out again. The blacks were filing out of an archway into another court. One of them was just placing something on a ledge of the further wall, and Conan saw it was the one who had tortured the boy. He was taller than the others, and wore a jeweled head-band. Of the Zingaran boy there was no trace. The giant followed his fellows, and presently Conan saw them emerge from the archway by which he had gained access to that castle of horror, and file away across the green slopes, in the direction from which he had come. They bore no arms, yet he felt that they planned further aggression against the Freebooters.

But before he went to warn the unsuspecting buccaneers, he wished to investigate the fate of the boy. No sound disturbed the quiet. The pirate believed that the towers and courts were deserted save for himself.

He went swiftly down the stair, crossed the court and passed through an arch into the court the blacks had just quitted. Now he saw the nature of the striated wall. It was banded by narrow ledges, apparently cut out of the solid stone, and ranged along these ledges or shelves were thousands of tiny figures, mostly grayish in color. These figures, not much longer than a man's hand, represented men, and so cleverly were they made that Conan recognized various racial characteristics in the different idols, features typical of Zingarans, Argoseans, Ophireans and Kushite corsairs. These last were black in color, just as their models were black in reality. Conan was aware of a vague uneasiness as he stared at the dumb sightless figures. There was a mimicry of reality about them that was somehow disturbing. He felt of them gingerly and could not decide of what material they were made. It felt like petrified bone; but he could not imagine petrified substance being found in the locality in such abundance as to be used so lavishly.

He noticed that the images representing types with which he was familiar were all on the higher ledges. The lower ledges were occupied by figures the features of which were strange to him. They either embodied merely the artists' imagination, or typified racial types long vanished and forgotten.

Shaking his head impatiently, Conan turned toward the pool. The circular court offered no place of concealment; as the body of the boy was nowhere in sight, it must be lying at the bottom of the pool.

Approaching the placid green disk, he stared into the glimmering surface. It was like looking through a thick green glass, unclouded, yet strangely illusory. Of no great dimensions, the pool was round as a well, bordered by a rim of green jade. Looking down he could see the rounded bottom—how far below the surface he could not decide. But the pool seemed incredibly deep—he was aware of a dizziness as he looked down, much as if he were looking into an abyss. He was puzzled by his ability to see the bottom; but it lay beneath his gaze, impossibly remote, illusive, shadowy, yet visible. At times he thought a faint luminosity was apparent deep in the jade-colored depth, but he could not be sure. Yet he was sure that the pool was empty except for the shimmering water.

Then where in the name of Crom was the boy whom he had seen brutally drowned in that pool? Rising, Conan fingered his sword, and gazed around the court again. His gaze focused on a spot on one of the higher ledges. There he had seen the tall black place something—cold sweat broke suddenly out on Conan's brown hide.

Hesitantly, yet as if drawn by a magnet, the pirate approached the shimmering wall. Dazed by a suspicion too monstrous to voice, he glared up at the last figure on that ledge. A horrible familiarity made itself evident. Stony, immobile, dwarfish, yet unmistakable, the features of the Zingaran boy stared unseeingly at him. Conan recoiled, shaken to his soul's foundations. His sword trailed in his paralyzed hand as he glared, open-mouthed, stunned by the realization which was too abysmal and awful for the mind to grasp.

Yet the fact was indisputable; the secret of the dwarfish figures was revealed, though behind that secret lay the darker and more cryptic secret of their being.

CHAPTER III

How long Conan stood drowned in dizzy cogitation, he never knew. A voice shook him out of his gaze, a feminine voice that shrieked more and more loudly, as if the owner of the voice were being borne nearer. Conan recognized that voice, and his paralysis vanished instantly.

A quick bound carried him high up on the narrow ledges, where he clung, kicking aside the clustering images to obtain room for his feet. Another spring and a scramble, and he was clinging to the rim of the wall, glaring over it. It was an outer wall; he was looking into the green meadow that surrounded the castle.

Across the grassy level a giant black was striding, carrying a squirming captive under one arm as a man might carry a rebellious child. It was Sancha, her black hair falling in disheveled rippling waves, her olive skin contrasting abruptly with the glossy ebony of her captor. He gave no heed to her wrigglings and cries as he made for the outer archway.

As he vanished within, Conan sprang recklessly down the wall and glided into the arch that opened into the further court. Crouching there, he saw the giant enter the court of the pool, carrying his writhing captive. Now he was able to make out the creature's details.

The superb symmetry of body and limbs was more impressive at close range. Under the ebon skin long, rounded muscles rippled, and Conan did not doubt that the monster could rend an ordinary man limb from limb. The nails of the fingers provided further weapons, for they were grown like the talons of a wild beast. The face was a carven ebony mask. The eyes' were tawny, a vibrant gold that glowed and glittered. But the face was inhuman; each line, each feature was stamped with evil—evil transcending the mere evil of humanity. The thing was not a human—it could not be; it was a growth of Life from the pits of blasphemous creation—a perversion of evolutionary development.

The giant cast Sancha down on the sward, where she grovelled, crying with pain and terror. He cast a glance about as if uncertain, and his tawny eyes narrowed as they rested on the images overturned and knocked from the wall. Then he stooped, grasped his captive by her neck and crotch, and strode purposefully toward the green pool. And Conan glided from his archway, and raced like a wind of death across the sward.

The giant wheeled, and his eyes flared as he saw the bronzed avenger rushing toward him. In the instant of surprize his cruel grip relaxed and Sancha wriggled from his hands and fell to the grass. The taloned hands spread and clutched, but Conan ducked beneath their swoop and drove his sword through the giant's groin. The black went down like a felled tree, gushing blood, and the next instant Conan was seized in a frantic grasp as Sancha sprang up and threw her arms around him in a frenzy of terror and hysterical relief.

He cursed as he disengaged himself, but his foe was already dead; the tawny eyes were glazed, the long ebony limbs had ceased to twitch.

"Oh, Conan," Sancha was sobbing, clinging tenaciously to him, "what will become of us? What are these monsters? Oh, surely this is hell and that was the devil-"

"Then hell needs a new devil." The Barachan grinned fiercely. "But how did he get hold of you? Have they taken the ship?"

"I don't know." She tried to wipe away her tears, fumbled for her skirt, and then remembered that she wore none. "I came ashore. I saw you follow Zaporavo, and I followed you both. I found Zaporavo—was—was it you who-"

"Who else?" he grunted. "What then?"

"I saw a movement in the trees," she shuddered. "I thought it was you. I called—then I saw that—that black thing squatting like an ape among the branches, leering down at me. It was like a nightmare; I couldn't run. All I could do was squeal. Then it dropped from the tree and seized me—oh, oh, oh!" She hid her face in her hands, and was shaken anew at the memory of the horror.

"Well, we've got to get out of here," he growled, catching her wrist. "Come on; we've got to get to the crew-"

"Most of them were asleep on the beach as I entered the woods," she said.

"Asleep?" he exclaimed profanely. "What in the seven devils of hell's fire and damnation-"

"Listen!" She froze, a white quivering image of fright.

"I heard it!" he snapped. "A moaning cry! Wait!"

He bounded up the ledges again and, glaring over the wall, swore with a concentrated fury that made even Sancha gasp. The black men were returning, but they came not alone or empty-handed. Each bore a limp human form; some bore two. Their captives were the Freebooters; they hung slackly in their captors' arms, and but for an occasional vague movement or twitching, Conan would have believed them dead. They had been disarmed but not stripped; one of the blacks bore their sheathed swords, a great armload of bristling steel. From time to time one of the seamen voiced a vague cry, like a drunkard calling out in sottish sleep.

Like a trapped wolf Conan glared about him. Three arches led out of the court of the pool. Through the eastern arch the blacks had left the court, and through it they would presumably return. He had entered by the southern arch. In the western arch he had hidden, and had not had time to notice what lay beyond it. Regardless of his ignorance of

32

the plan of the castle, he was forced to make his decision promptly.

Springing down the wall, he replaced the images with frantic haste, dragged the corpse of his victim to the pool and cast it in. It sank instantly and, as he looked, he distinctly saw an appalling contraction—a shrinking, a hardening. He hastily turned away, shuddering. Then he seized his companion's arm and led her hastily toward the southern archway, while she begged to be told what was happening.

"They've bagged the crew," he answered hastily. "I haven't any plan, but we'll hide somewhere and watch. If they don't look in the pool, they may not suspect our presence."

"But they'll see the blood on the grass!"

"Maybe they'll think one of their own devils spilled it," he answered. "Anyway, we'll have to take the chance."

They were in the court from which he had watched the torture of the boy, and he led her hastily up the stair that mounted the southern wall, and forced her into a crouching position behind the balustrade of the balcony; it was poor concealment, but the best they could do.

Scarcely had they settled themselves, when the blacks filed into the court. There was a resounding clash at the foot of the stairs, and Conan stiffened, grasping his sword. But the blacks passed through an archway on the southwestern side, and they heard a series of thuds and groans. The giants were casting their victims down on the sward. An hysterical giggle rose to Sancha's lips, and Conan quickly clapped his hand over her mouth, stifling the sound before it could betray them.

After a while they heard the padding of many feet on the sward below, and then silence reigned. Conan peered over the wall. The court was empty. The blacks were once more gathered about the pool in the adjoining court, squatting on their haunches. They seemed to pay no heed to the great smears of blood on the sward and the jade rim of the pool. Evidently blood stains were nothing unusual. Nor were they looking into the pool. They were engrossed in some inexplicable conclave of their own; the tall black was playing again on his golden pipes, and his companions listened like ebony statues.

Taking Sancha's hand, Conan glided down the stair, stooping so that his head would not be visible above the wall. The cringing girl followed perforce, staring fearfully at the arch that let into the court of the pool, but through which, at that angle, neither the pool nor its grim throng were visible. At the foot of the stair lay the swords of the Zingarans. The clash they had heard had been the casting down of the captured weapons.

Conan drew Sancha toward the southwestern arch, and they silently crossed the sward and entered the court beyond. There the Freebooters lay in careless heaps, mustaches bristling, earrings glinting. Here and there one stirred or groaned restlessly. Conan bent down to them, and Sancha knelt beside him, leaning forward with her hands on her thighs.

"What is that sweet cloying smell?" she asked nervously. "It's on all their breaths."

"It's that damned fruit they were eating," he answered softly. "I remember the smell of it. It must have been like the black lotus, that makes men sleep. By Crom, they are beginning to awake—but they're unarmed, and I have an idea that those black devils won't wait long before they begin their magic on them. What chance will the lads have, unarmed and stupid with slumber?"

He brooded for an instant, scowling with the intentness of his thoughts; then seized Sancha's olive shoulder in a grip that made her wince.

"Listen! I'll draw those black swine into another part of the castle and keep them busy for a while. Meanwhile you shake these fools awake, and bring their swords to them—it's a fighting chance. Can you do it?"

"I—I—don't know!" she stammered, shaking with terror, and hardly knowing what she was saying.

With a curse, Conan caught her thick tresses near her head and shook her until the walls danced to her dizzy sight.

"You must do it!" he hissed at her. "It's our only chance!"

"I'll do my best!" she gasped, and with a grunt of commendation and an encouraging slap on the back that nearly knocked her down, he glided away.

A few moments later he was crouching at the arch that opened into the court of the pool, glaring upon his enemies. They still sat about the pool, but were beginning to show evidences of an evil impatience. From the court where lay the rousing buccaneers he heard their groans growing louder, beginning to be mingled with incoherent curses. He tensed his muscles and sank into a pantherish crouch, breathing easily between his teeth.

The jeweled giant rose, taking his pipes from his lips— and at that instant Conan was among the startled blacks with a tigerish bound. And as a tiger leaps and strikes among his prey, Conan leaped and struck: thrice his blade flickered before any could lift a hand in defense; then he bounded from among them and raced across the sward. Behind him sprawled three black figures, their skulls split.

But though the unexpected fury of his surprize had caught the giants off guard, the survivors recovered quickly enough. They were at his heels as he ran through the western arch, their long legs sweeping them over the ground at headlong speed. However, he felt confident of his ability to outfoot them at will; but that was not his purpose. He intended leading them on a long chase, in order to give Sancha time to rouse and arm the Zingarans.

36

And as he raced into the court beyond the western arch, he swore. This court differed from the others he had seen. Instead of being round, it was octagonal, and the arch by which he had entered was the only entrance or exit.

Wheeling, he saw that the entire band had followed him in; a group clustered in the arch, and the rest spread out in a wide line as they approached. He faced them, backing slowly toward the northern wall. The line bent into a semicircle, spreading out to hem him in. He continued to move backward, but more and more slowly, noting the spaces widening between the pursuers. They feared lest he should try to dart around a horn of the crescent, and lengthened their line to prevent it.

He watched with the calm alertness of a wolf, and when he struck it was with the devastating suddenness of a thunderbolt—full at the center of the crescent. The giant who barred his way went down cloven to the middle of the breast-bone, and the pirate was outside their closing ring before the blacks to right and left could come to their stricken comrade's aid. The group at the gate prepared to receive his onslaught, but Conan did not charge them. He had turned and was watching his hunters without apparent emotion, and certainly without fear.

This time they did not spread out in a thin line. They had learned that it was fatal to divide their forces against such an incarnation of clawing, rending fury. They bunched up in a compact mass, and advanced on him without undue haste, maintaining their formation.

Conan knew that if he fell foul of that mass of taloned muscle and bone, there could be but one culmination. Once let them drag him down among them where they could reach him with their talons and use their greater body-weight to advantage, even his primitive ferocity would not prevail. He glanced around the wall and saw a ledge-like projection above a corner on the western side. What it was he did not know, but it would serve his purpose. He began backing toward that corner, and the giants advanced more rapidly. They evidently thought that they were herding him into the corner themselves, and Conan found time to reflect that they probably looked on him as a member of a lower order, mentally inferior to themselves. So much the better. Nothing is more disastrous than underestimating one's antagonist.

Now he was only a few yards from the wall, and the blacks were closing in rapidly, evidently thinking to pin him in the corner before he realized his situation. The group at the gate had deserted their post and were hastening to join their fellows. The giants half-crouched, eyes blazing like golden hell-fire, teeth glistening whitely, taloned hands lifted as if to fend off attack. They expected an abrupt and violent move on the part of their prey, but when it came, it took them by surprize.

Conan lifted his sword, took a step toward them, then wheeled and raced to the wall. With a fleeting coil and release of steel muscles, he shot high in the air, and his straining arm hooked its fingers over the projection. Instantly there was a rending crash and the jutting ledge gave way, precipitating the pirate back into the court.

He hit on his back, which for all its springy sinews would have broken but for the cushioning of the sward, and rebounding like a great cat, he faced his foes. The dancing recklessness was gone from his eyes. They blazed like blue bale-fire; his mane bristled, his thin lips snarled. In an instant the affair had changed from a daring game to a battle of life and death, and Conan's savage nature responded with all the fury of the wild.

The blacks, halted an instant by the swiftness of the episode, now made to sweep on him and drag him down. But in that instant a shout broke the stillness. Wheeling, the giants saw a disreputable throng crowding the arch. The buccaneers weaved drunkenly, they swore incoherently; they were addled and bewildered, but they grasped their swords and advanced with a ferocity not dimmed in the slightest by the fact that they did not understand what it was all about.

As the blacks glared in amazement, Conan yelled stridently and struck them like a razor-edged thunderbolt. They fell like ripe grains beneath his blade, and the Zingarans, shouting with muddled fury, ran groggily across the court and fell on their gigantic foes with bloodthirsty zeal. They were still dazed; emerging hazily from drugged slumber, they had felt Sancha frantically shaking them and shoving swords into their fists, and had vaguely heard her urging them to some sort of action. They had not understood all she said, but the sight of strangers, and blood streaming, was enough for them.

In an instant the court was turned into a battle-ground which soon resembled a slaughter-house. The Zingarans weaved and rocked on their feet, but they wielded their swords with power and effect, swearing prodigiously, and quite oblivious to all wounds except those instantly fatal. They far outnumbered the blacks, but these proved themselves no mean antagonists. Towering above their assailants, the giants wrought havoc with talons and teeth, tearing out men's throats, and dealing blows with clenched fists that crushed in skulls. Mixed and mingled in that melee, the buccaneers could not use their superior agility to the best advantage, and many were too stupid from their drugged sleep to avoid blows aimed at them. They fought with a blind wild-beast ferocity, too intent on dealing death to evade it. The sound of the hacking swords was like that of butchers' cleavers, and the shrieks, yells and curses were appalling.

Sancha, shrinking in the archway, was stunned by the noise and fury; she got a dazed impression of a whirling chaos in which steel flashed and hacked, arms tossed, snarling faces appeared and vanished, and straining bodies collided, rebounded, locked and mingled in a devil's dance of madness.

Details stood out briefly, like black etchings on a background of blood. She saw a Zingaran sailor, blinded by a great flap of scalp torn loose and hanging over his eyes, brace his straddling legs and drive his sword to the hilt in a black belly. She distinctly heard the buccaneer grunt as he struck, and saw the victim's tawny eyes roll up in sudden agony; blood and entrails gushed out over the driven blade. The dying black caught the blade with his naked hands, and the sailor tugged blindly and stupidly; then a black arm hooked about the Zingaran's head, a black knee was planted with cruel force in the middle of his back. His head was jerked back at a terrible angle, and something cracked above the noise of the fray, like the breaking of a thick branch. The conqueror dashed his victim's body to the earth—and as he did, something like a beam of blue light flashed across his shoulders from behind, from right to left. He staggered, his head toppled forward on his breast, and thence, hideously, to the earth.

Sancha turned sick. She gagged and wished to vomit. She made abortive efforts to turn and flee from the spectacle, but her legs would not work. Nor could she close her eyes. In fact, she opened them wider. Revolted, repelled, nauseated, yet she felt the awful fascination she had always experienced at sight of blood. Yet this battle transcended anything she had ever seen fought out between human beings in port raids or sea battles. Then she saw Conan.

Separated from his mates by the whole mass of the enemy, Conan had been enveloped in a black wave of arms and bodies, and dragged down. Then they would quickly have stamped the life out of him, but he had pulled down one of them with him, and the black's body protected that of the pirate beneath him. They kicked and tore at the Barachan and dragged at their writhing comrade, but Conan's teeth were set desperately in his throat, and the pirate clung tenaciously to his dying shield.

An onslaught of Zingarans caused a slackening of the press, and Conan threw aside the corpse and rose, blood-smeared and terrible. The giants towered above him like great black shadows, clutching, buffeting the air with terrible blows. But he was as hard to hit or grapple as a blood-mad panther, and at every turn or flash of his blade, blood jetted. He had already taken punishment enough to kill three ordinary men, but his bull-like vitality was undiminished.

His war cry rose above the medley of the carnage, and the bewildered but furious Zingarans took fresh heart and redoubled their strokes, until the rending of flesh and the crunching of bone beneath the swords almost drowned the howls of pain and wrath.

The blacks wavered, and broke for the gate, and Sancha squealed at their coming and scurried out of the way. They jammed in the narrow archway, and the Zingarans stabbed and hacked at their straining backs with strident yelps of glee. The gate was a shambles before the survivors broke through and scattered, each for himself.

The battle became a chase. Across grassy courts, up shimmering stairs, over the slanting roofs of fantastic towers, even along the broad coping of the walls, the giants fled, dripping blood at each step, harried by their merciless pursuers as by wolves. Cornered, some of them turned at bay and men died. But the ultimate result was always the same—a mangled black body twitching on the sward, or hurled writhing and twisting from parapet or tower roof.

Sancha had taken refuge in the court of the pool, where she crouched, shaking with terror. Outside rose a fierce yelling, feet pounded the sward, and through the arch burst a black, red-stained figure. It was the giant who wore the gemmed headband. A squat pursuer was close behind, and the black turned, at the very brink of the pool. In his extremity he had picked up a sword dropped by a dying sailor, and as the Zingaran rushed recklessly at him, he struck with the unfamiliar weapon. The buccaneer dropped with his skull crushed, but so awkwardly the blow was dealt, the blade shivered in the giant's hand.

He hurled the hilt at the figures which thronged the arch, and bounded toward the pool, his face a convulsed mask of hate.

Conan burst through the men at the gate, and his feet spurned the sward in his headlong charge.

But the giant threw his great arms wide and from his lips rang an inhuman cry—the only sound made by a black during the entire fight. It screamed to the sky its awful hate; it was like a voice howling from the pits. At the sound the Zingarans faltered and hesitated. But Conan did not pause. Silently and murderously he drove at the ebon figure poised on the brink of the pool.

But even as his dripping sword gleamed in the air, the black wheeled and bounded high. For a flash of an instant they saw him poised in midair above the pool; then with an earth-shaking roar, the green waters rose and rushed up to meet him, enveloping him in a green volcano.

Conan checked his headlong rush just in time to keep from toppling into the pool, and he sprang back, thrusting his men behind him with mighty swings of his arms. The green pool was like a geyser now, the noise rising to deafening volume as the great column of water reared and reared, blossoming at the crest with a great crown of foam.

Conan was driving his men to the gate, herding them ahead of him, beating them with the flat of his sword; the roar of the water-spout seemed to have robbed them of their faculties. Seeing Sancha standing paralyzed, staring with wide-eyed terror at the seething pillar, he accosted her with a bellow that cut through the thunder of the water and made her jump out of her daze. She ran to him, arms outstretched, and he caught her up under one arm and raced out of the court.

In the court which opened on the outer world, the survivors had gathered, weary, tattered, wounded and blood-stained, and stood gaping dumbly at the great unstable pillar that towered momentarily nearer the blue vault of the sky. Its green trunk was laced with white; its foaming crown was thrice the circumference of its base. Momentarily it threatened to burst and fall in an engulfing torrent, yet it continued to jet skyward.

Conan's eyes swept the bloody, naked group, and he cursed to see only a score. In the stress of the moment he grasped a corsair by the neck and shook him so violently that blood from the man's wounds spattered all near them.

"Where are the rest?" he bellowed in his victim's ear.

"That's all!" the other yelled back, above the roar of the geyser. "The others were all killed by those black-"

"Well, get out of here!" roared Conan, giving him a thrust that sent him staggering headlong toward the outer archway. "That fountain is going to burst in a moment-"

"We'll all be drowned!" squawked a Freebooter, limping toward the arch.

"Drowned, hell!" yelled Conan. "We'll be turned to pieces of petrified bone! Get out, blast you!"

He ran to the outer archway, one eye on the green roaring tower that loomed so awfully above him, the other on stragglers. Dazed with blood-lust, fighting, and the thunderous noise, some of the Zingarans moved like men in a trance. Conan hurried them up; his method was simple. He grasped loiterers by the scruff of the neck, impelled them violently through the gate, added impetus with a lusty kick in the rear, spicing his urgings for haste with pungent comments on the victim's ancestry. Sancha showed an inclination to remain with him, but he jerked away her twining arms, blaspheming luridly, and accelerated her movements with a tremendous slap on the posterior that sent her scurrying across the plateau.

Conan did not leave the gate until he was sure all his men who yet lived were out of the castle and started across the level meadow. Then he glanced again at the roaring pillar looming against the sky, dwarfing the towers, and he too fled that castle of nameless horrors.

The Zingarans had already crossed the rim of the plateau and were fleeing down the slopes. Sancha waited for him at the crest of the first slope beyond the rim, and there he paused for an instant to look back at the castle. It was as if a gigantic green-stemmed and white-blossomed flower swayed above the towers; the roar filled the sky. Then the jade-green and snowy pillar broke with a noise like the rending of the skies, and walls and towers were blotted out in a thunderous torrent.

Conan caught the girl's hand, and fled. Slope after slope rose and fell before them, and behind sounded the rushing of a river. A glance over his straining shoulder showed a broad green ribbon rising and falling as it swept over the slopes. The torrent had not spread out and dissipated; like a giant serpent it flowed over the depressions and the rounded crests. It held a consistent course—it was following them.

The realization roused Conan to a greater pitch of endurance. Sancha stumbled and went to her knees with a moaning cry of despair and exhaustion. Catching her up, Conan tossed her over his giant shoulder and ran on. His breast heaved, his knees trembled; his breath tore in great gasps through his teeth. He reeled in his gait. Ahead of him he saw the sailors toiling, spurred on by the terror that gripped them.

The ocean burst suddenly on his view, and in his swimming gaze floated the Wastrel, unharmed. Men tumbled into the boats helter-skelter. Sancha fell into the bottom and lay there in a crumpled heap. Conan, though the blood thundered in his ears and the world swam red to his gaze, took an oar with the panting sailors.

With hearts ready to burst from exhaustion, they pulled for the ship. The green river burst through the fringe of trees. Those trees fell as if their stems had been cut away, and as they sank into the jade-colored flood, they vanished. The tide flowed out over the beach, lapped at the ocean, and the waves turned a deeper, more sinister green.

Unreasoning, instinctive fear held the buccaneers, making them urge their agonized bodies and reeling brains to greater effort; what they feared they knew not, but they did know that in that abominable smooth green ribbon was a menace to body and to soul. Conan knew, and as he saw the broad line slip into the waves and stream through the water toward them, without altering its shape or course, he called up his last ounce of reserve strength so fiercely that the oar snapped in his hands.

But their prows bumped against the timbers of the Wastrel, and the sailors staggered up the chains, leaving the boats to drift as they would. Sancha went up on Conan's broad shoulder, hanging limp as a corpse, to be dumped unceremoniously on to the deck as the Barachan took the wheel, gasping orders to his skeleton of a crew. Throughout the affair, he had taken the lead without question, and they had instinctively followed him. They reeled about like drunken men, fumbling mechanically at ropes and braces. The anchor chain, unshackled, splashed into the water, the sails unfurled and bellied in a rising wind. The Wastrel quivered and shook herself, and swung majestically seaward. Conan glared shoreward; like a tongue of emerald flame, a ribbon licked out on the water futilely, an oar's length from the Wastrel's keel. It advanced no further. From that end of the tongue, his gaze followed an unbroken stream of lambent green, across the white beach, and over the slopes, until it faded in the blue distance.

The Barachan, regaining his wind, grinned at the panting crew. Sancha was standing near him, hysterical tears coursing down her cheeks. Conan's breeks hung in blood-stained tatters; his girdle and sheath were gone, his sword, driven upright into the deck beside him, was notched and crusted with red. Blood thickly clotted his black mane, and one ear had been half torn from his head. His arms, legs, breast and shoulders were bitten and clawed as if by panthers. But he grinned as he braced his powerful legs, and swung on the wheel in sheer exuberance of muscular might.

"What now?" faltered the girl.

"The plunder of the seas!" he laughed. "A paltry crew, and that chewed and clawed to pieces, but they can work the ship, and crews can always be found. Come here, girl, and give me a kiss."

"A kiss?" she cried hysterically. "You think of kisses at a time like this?"

His laughter boomed above the snap and thunder of the sails, as he caught her up off her feet in the crook of one mighty arm, and smacked her red lips with resounding relish.

"I think of Life!" he roared. "The dead are dead, and what has passed is done! I have a ship and a fighting crew and a girl with lips like wine, and that's all I ever asked. Lick your wounds, bullies, and break out a cask of ale. You're going to work ship as she never was worked before. Dance and sing while you buckle to it, damn you! To the devil with empty seas! We're bound for waters where the seaports are fat, and the merchant ships are crammed with plunder!"